So, here's the thing . . .
I'm a bad drawer.

Like, *real* bad.

I've practiced.
And practiced.
But it's like my hands
can't hear my brain.

Don't believe me?
All right, let me show you.
Wait . . .

You're not going to laugh, are you?

Don't laugh, OK?

...OK????

see?

The only thing I know how
to draw is a pine tree,
but that's because it's
basically a scribble.

I can play soccer pretty OK.

And I make the best cookies.

And I know I'm good at math.

I'm just a really
bad drawer.

But the thing is, I have this adventure in my head . . .

It's about a mouse named Bailey

who rides a half-cat half-bird

named Catbird,

and how they save

the mouse kingdom

from invading

wand-wielding

dragons!

Check.
It.
Out.

Well . . .
um . . .
that's not *exactly* how I imagined it . . .

ARGH

I just wish I could draw
like some of my friends.

Tillie—who's always doodling in journals—is so good at drawing amazing enormous skyscrapers and scenery. She'd create such incredible worlds for Bailey.

Oh! And Jessixa—who's always dancing and skipping and awesomely spells her name with an x—decorates her own outfits. She'd do the BEST costumes for the mice!

My *other* friend Jessica can draw letters almost like they are museum pieces . . . She could be the kingdom's calligrapher!

And Anna—who's always listening
to music I have never heard
before—creates the realest-looking
birds and the most amazing cats.

Also, Armand's always designing
his own toys to play with. What if
he made Bailey's hot-air balloon?!

Even my little brother Ethan draws dragons better than me . . .

See?!?

Hmph.

HEY,
wait a
minute!

What if I ask them to help me?
And in exchange,
I bake them some cookies?
With our powers combined
we could make

the coolest Catbird!

That way I can actually *show* you how Bailey steals the wand

from the chief dragon

and conjures an incredible hot-air balloon

that Catbird uses
to fly everyone

from the mouse kingdom

away to

Maybe my stories *are* good enough.
I just need some help telling them.
All I had to do was ask. Now my friends
and I can share our story with . . .

WORLD!

Just like Bailey and
Catbird would want it.
The MOUSE KINGDOM
SAFETY!

Now Catbird needs a theme song.

But there's only one problem . . .

I'm a *really* bad singer . . .

ABOUT THE ILLUSTRATORS

JESSIXA BAGLEY is a children's book author and illustrator of the 2016 SCBWI Golden Kite Award-winning *Boats for Papa* and the 2018 Ezra Jack Keats Honor-winning *Laundry Day*.

ARMAND BALTAZAR is a visual development artist, art director, and illustrator, who's currently working on an epic illustrated middle-grade adventure series, Timeless, for HarperCollins Publishers.

ANNA BOND is cofounder and chief creative officer at Rifle Paper Co., a stationery, home, and lifestyle brand based on Anna's hand-painted designs.

TRAVIS FOSTER is an illustrator whose work has been published by Disney, Rodale Press, Simon & Schuster, *Forbes*, the *Wall Street Journal*, and the *Washington Post*.

JESSICA HISCHE is a letterer, illustrator, type designer, and *New York Times* best-selling children's book author of *Tomorrow I'll Be Brave* and *Tomorrow I'll Be Kind*.

TILLIE WALDEN is a cartoonist and illustrator who won the 2018 Eisner Award for Best Reality-Based Work for her graphic novel *Spinning*.

ETHAN YOUNG is an Eisner Award-nominated cartoonist, best known for *Nanjing: The Burning City*, winner of the 2016 Reuben Award for Best Graphic Novel.

PENGUIN WORKSHOP
An imprint of Penguin Random House LLC, New York

First published in the United States of America by Penguin Workshop, an imprint of Penguin Random House LLC, New York, 2022

Photo credits: pages 20–25 (notebooks, paper) from Getty Images

Visit us online at penguinrandomhouse.com.

Library of Congress Cataloging-in-Publication Data is available.

Manufactured in China

ISBN 9780593385784 10 9 8 7 6 5 4 3 2 1 HH

Design by Lynn Portnoff